George

Based on *The Railway Series* by the Rev. W. Awdry

Illustrations by
Robin Davies

EGMONT

EGMONT

We bring stories to life

First published in Great Britain in 2006
by Egmont UK Limited
239 Kensington High Street, London W8 6SA
This edition published in 2008
All Rights Reserved

Thomas the Tank Engine & Friends™

CREATED BY BRITT ALLCROFT

Based on the Railway Series by the Reverend W Awdry
© 2008 Gullane (Thomas) LLC. A HIT Entertainment company.
Thomas the Tank Engine & Friends and Thomas & Friends are trademarks of Gullane (Thomas) Limited.
Thomas the Tank Engine & Friends and Design is Reg. U.S. Pat. & Tm. Off.

HiT entertainment

ISBN 978 1 4052 3479 5
1 3 5 7 9 10 8 6 4 2
Printed in Italy

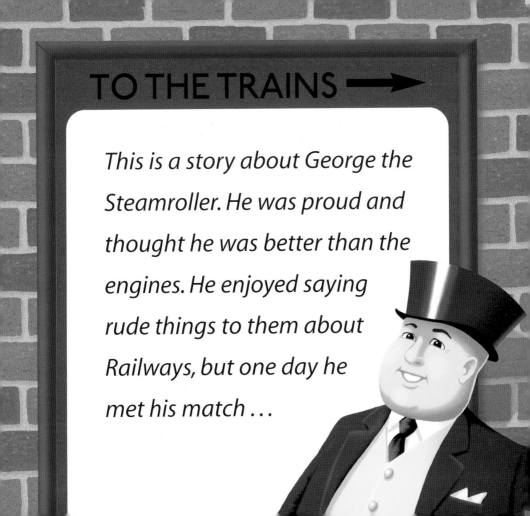

TO THE TRAINS ➡

This is a story about George the Steamroller. He was proud and thought he was better than the engines. He enjoyed saying rude things to them about Railways, but one day he met his match …

One summer, workmen brought George the steamroller to work on the road next to The Thin Controller's station. The road was being widened, so the workmen took down the wall between the rails and the road.

George didn't think much of Railways or steam engines, so whenever he saw an engine travelling past, he made loud, rude comments about the Railway.

Sir Handel hadn't met George yet. His wheels had been slipping between the rails so The Thin Controller sent him away to be fitted with new wheels with broader tyres. When Sir Handel came back, the other engines teased him saying he had steamroller wheels!

"With my new wheels I'll be able to go faster than any of you," Sir Handel said, boastfully.

The engines couldn't wait to see what would happen when arrogant Sir Handel met rude George the steamroller.

That night, the engines told Sir Handel about the things George had said to them.

"He called us worn-out wheels on worn-out rails!" Rheneas said, sadly.

"And he said that Railways are no good, so he should pull them all up and make them into roads," Peter Sam added, in horror.

"But with your grand new wheels, you're just the engine to tackle George," Skarloey said.

Sir Handel felt very important. "Don't worry," he replied, grandly. "I'll show him who's best!"

The next morning, Sir Handel met George at the level crossing.

"So *you're* Sir Handel," George said, casually. "I've heard that you swank around with your new steamroller wheels trying to be as good as me!"

Sir Handel smiled. "Actually," he said, "I'm *better* than you!" and he puffed smugly away.

George was furious. He didn't like an engine to get the better of him.

A few days later, Sir Handel was delivering a special load to the station. As he approached, he saw George slowly rolling along right next to the track.

"Peep-pip-peep!" Sir Handel whistled loudly, but George ignored him.

George was so close to the track, that there was barely room for Sir Handel to get past.

"Peeeep-pip-pip-peeeeep!" Sir Handel whistled angrily. "Get out of my way, you clumsy great road-hog."

"I won't be ordered around by an imitation steamroller," George retorted, proudly.

"Imitation steamroller?" Sir Handel shouted, crossly. "*I'm* no imitation of anyone! You obviously wish *you* were an engine, otherwise you wouldn't be travelling so close to the rails!"

The two of them travelled side by side, exchanging insults as they went.

No one could explain what happened next. George's Driver said he signalled for Sir Handel to stop, and Sir Handel's Driver said he signalled for George to stop, but suddenly it all went wrong!

There was a loud crash as George's front roller hit Sir Handel's brake-van, which tilted sideways on the track. Sir Handel's Fireman went to the station to get help. George and Sir Handel stood in shocked silence whilst their Drivers argued about whose fault it all was.

A policeman arrived just in time to stop the Drivers' argument ending in fisticuffs! Soon after, The Thin Controller arrived with Rusty and the Fireman to settle the matter.

"I expected more from *both* of you," The Thin Controller said to Sir Handel and George. "Your silly quarrelling has caused chaos and delay!"

Sir Handel and George were sorry. They now realised that their feuding had caused trouble.

Luckily they hadn't been going fast enough to cause any damage. Once George had backed away, Rusty was coupled to Sir Handel. They moved carefully forward so the brake van tilted back on to the track. Then they hurried on to the station to deliver the special load.

"Come on, George, we should get going, too," said his Driver. "We're starting a new job tomorrow on the other side of the Island."

George smiled. "It's a shame we're leaving," he said. "Having seen the engines working together in a crisis, I've decided that they're not so bad after all!"

In the engine shed that night, Sir Handel told the engines about the crash. Being a boastful engine he exaggerated the story, telling them that it was nearly a terrible disaster and that it was only his quick thinking that had saved them.

"Wow!" said Rheneas, in admiration. "It sounds like you really showed George who's best!"

Rusty knew the real story, but he kept quiet to let Sir Handel have his moment of glory.

The next day, the road was finished and the workmen put up a fence between the road and the tracks. When Sir Handel heard that George had gone, he was more conceited than ever and told all the engines that *he* had made him go away.

Rusty decided it was about time that Sir Handel was brought down a peg or two, so he told the other engines what had really happened that day.

Suddenly Sir Handel was being laughed at wherever he went. The engines said he needed his steamroller wheels to balance his big head!

Sir Handel had learnt a valuable lesson.
He would never again make up silly stories just to make him sound more important. And a few months later, when he met George again, they had a good chat about roads and Railways and decided that they could be friends after all!

The Thomas Story Library is THE definitive collection of stories about Thomas and ALL his friends.

5 more Thomas Story Library titles will be chuffing into your local bookshop in August 2008!

Jeremy
Hector
BoCo
Billy
Whiff

And there are even more Thomas Story Library books to follow late

So go on, start your Thomas Story Library NOW!

A Fantastic Offer for Thomas the Tank Engine Fans!

STICK
POUND
COIN
HERE

In every Thomas Story Library book like this one, you will find a special token. Collect 6 Thomas tokens and we will send you a brilliant Thomas poster, and a double-sided bedroom door hanger! Simply tape a £1 coin in the space above, and fill out the form overleaf.

TO BE COMPLETED BY AN ADULT

To apply for this great offer, ask an adult to complete the coupon below and send it with a pound coin and 6 tokens, to:
THOMAS OFFERS, PO BOX 715, HORSHAM RH12 5WG

☐ Please send a Thomas poster and door hanger. I enclose 6 tokens plus a £1 coin. (Price includes P&P)

Fan's name..

Address..

....Postcode..............................

Date of birth..

Name of parent/guardian...

Signature of parent/guardian..